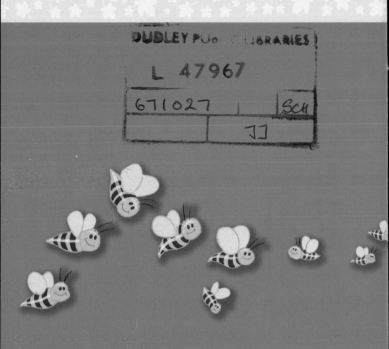

Published by Ladybird Books Ltd
A Penguin Company
Penguin Books Ltd, 80 Strand, London, WC2R 0RL, England
Penguin Books Australia Ltd, Camberwell, Victoria, Australia
Penguin Group (NZ), cnr Airborne and Rosedale Roads, Albany, Auckland 1310, New Zealand

Copyright © Disney 2005
Based on the Pooh stories by A.A. Milne
(Copyright the Pooh Properties Trust)

All rights reserved

2 4 6 8 10 9 7 5 3 1

LADYBIRD and the device of a ladybird are trademarks of Ladybird Books Ltd

Disney

Pooh's Daily Hums

Ladybird

Wake-up time

As soon as the sunshine says hello,
Pooh Bear makes his bed.
He wiggles his nose
and touches his toes,
and sings little songs in his head.

Playtime

In the middle of the morning
Pooh goes out to play.
He has a swing,
pretends he's king,
and looks forward to his day.

Lunchtime

Every single day at noon
Pooh Bear eats his honey.
Sometimes he slurps,
and then he burps.
He always thinks that's funny!

Craft time

Some days after eating lunch,
Pooh has a craft to start.
He paints a flower
for a happy hour.
It's fun to make art.

Nap time

Every sleepy afternoon
Pooh Bear takes a nap.
He dreams of things
with whistles and wings
that go "rap–a–tap–tap, a–tap–tap."

Dinner time

While the sun is still awake,
Pooh sits down to eat.
He says a blessing
about honey dressing
and a world so sunny and sweet.

Story time

Just before the sun disappears
Pooh turns on the light.
He looks at books
about princes and crooks
and things that go bump
in the night.

Bath time

Every night when it gets dark
Pooh climbs into the tub.
He cleans his ears
so he can hear
and sings,
"Rub-dub-rub-dub-rub-dub."

Bed time

When the sky is full of stars
Pooh Bear goes to sleep.
He closes his eyes
and wonders why
his head is full of sheep!

Snooze time

Winnie the Pooh is dreaming
about the friends he misses.
He's dreaming of happy times
and nice good-night kisses.

Sleepy time

Pooh is laughing and singing,
and humming a dreamy hum.
And in his dream he's wishing
that morning soon will come.

Dream time

Winnie the Pooh is sleeping,
so you close your tired eyes, too!
Catch up with your dreams –
Pooh's waiting there for you.